SOLO

PAUL GERAGHTY

Mini Treasures

RED FOX

To the high-flying businessman
and her cat

SOLO
A RED FOX BOOK 978 0 09 944769 6

First published in Great Britain in 1995 by Hutchinson Children's Books,
an imprint of Random House Children's Books

Red Fox Mini Treasures edition published 2002

5 7 9 10 8 6 4

Copyright © Paul Geraghty 1995

The right of Paul Geraghty to be identified as the author and illustrator of this work has
been asserted in accordance with the Copyright, Designs and Patents Act 1988

All rights reserved. No part of this publication may be reproduced, stored in a retrieval
system, or transmitted in any form or by any means, electronic, mechanical, photocopying,
recording or otherwise, without the prior permission of the publishers.

Red Fox Books are published by Random House Children's Books,
61-63 Uxbridge Road, London W5 5SA,
a division of The Random House Group Ltd,
in Australia by Random House Australia (Pty) Ltd,
20 Alfred Street, Milsons Point, Sydney, NSW 2061, Australia,
in New Zealand by Random House New Zealand Ltd,
18 Poland Road, Glenfield, Auckland 10, New Zealand,
and in South Africa by Random House (Pty) Ltd,
Endulini, 5A Jubilee Road, Parktown 2193, South Africa

THE RANDOM HOUSE GROUP Limited Reg. No. 954009

www.paulgeraghty.net

A CIP catalogue record for this book is available from the British Library.

Printed in China

In the dark of winter,
Floe leapt out of the sea.

For days she hiked across the ice. It blew and it snowed. She slid and she stumbled, but she never once stopped to rest.

Sometimes she tobogganed; often she had to climb.

She was on her way to meet her mate Fin.

Just as the struggle began to seem endless,
Floe's heart quickened. She could hear a
great noise in the distance.

Up ahead, the horizon was dark with
penguins as they gathered in their thousands.
The colony grew and grew as more arrived
each minute. She was nearly home.

Floe bustled through the rookery, calling for Fin.

If he'd survived the months at sea, he would be out there somewhere looking for her too.

For hours she called. Then, far away in the forest of noise, she thought she heard him. She called, then listened. Faintly, his voice echoed back. It was Fin!

Floe called again. Fin replied. She followed
the sound she knew so well.

And there he was at last. They bowed
and stretched in delight. They touched
chests. Fin led Floe on a celebration walk.
They were together again.

A few weeks later, their voices sang out
with pride. Floe had laid her egg.
She passed it to Fin.

He took it onto his feet,
gently covered it from
the cold and prepared for
the long, hungry wait.

Again they sang and then Floe was gone – on the big journey back to the sea to collect food for the baby.

At the water's edge she hesitated. She was desperate to swim, but something made her stop.

Then she saw it…

… a leopard seal! Just beneath the ice, ready to snatch her as she dived in. Floe stood still and waited.

Eventually, the seal flicked the surface and set off, looking for less careful penguins to hunt.

Floe splashed into the clear water and twisted down into the deep.

Back in the rookery, Fin huddled with the other penguins. For three bitter months he had been without food and still he protected the egg.

Then, one morning the egg began to crack. Fin watched in wonder as the shell broke open and the baby was born. The first thing baby Solo saw was a winter storm.

Floe wasn't back from the sea, so Fin fed her what little oil he had.

Excitement grew as the first fat females returned. All around them, other chicks were starting to hatch.

At last Floe arrived. The sight of Fin with baby Solo filled her with joy. She bowed and bumped against Fin. He passed her the baby. They showed cheeks and sang, and Solo got her first good meal of squid.

Then, desperate with hunger,
Fin set straight off for the sea.
It was his turn to collect the food.
   He splashed with delight.
He tumbled and swam. For weeks
he dived and fished.

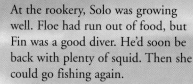

At the rookery, Solo was growing well. Floe had run out of food, but Fin was a good diver. He'd soon be back with plenty of squid. Then she could go fishing again.

One morning Floe and Solo saw dark shapes approaching in the distance – fat, waddling penguins! They could hardly wait.

But Fin wasn't among the first ones back. They could only watch as all around them chicks were fed and hungry mothers were finally free to go to sea.

Each time more penguins arrived, their spirits rose. But still Fin didn't come.

Days passed. Anxiously, they watched as the last few stragglers came home. Perhaps Fin had got lost? Or perhaps he'd gone farther than the others to find good food?

Solo cried with hunger, but Floe had nothing left to feed her. She was hungry too. And now there were no more shapes in the distance to give them hope.

Floe waited one more day. And when Fin didn't come, she knew she would have to leave her chick or they would both starve.

She put Solo on the snow, looked back once then hurried off towards the sea. It was a faint hope, but perhaps she could make the trip in time to save her chick.

Solo tried to follow, but she couldn't keep up. She waited quietly for a while, but then she cried out from the cold.

A few heads turned. Some of the penguins noticed that Solo was on her own.

One penguin tried to drag her onto his feet, but another pulled her from behind. A third tugged at her flipper. Suddenly, five large penguins were fighting over Solo. They all wanted to care for her, but they tugged and nipped so hard that she cried out in fright.

Scurrying away, Solo slid down a crevice. At the bottom she lay awhile, panting with shock.

Curious faces peered down at her. At least she was safe from their jabbing beaks.

Slowly she recovered, and soon had the strength to struggle along the bottom.
At one end, the space opened up and Solo found herself at the edge of the rookery.
From there, she set off to find her mother.

She hadn't gone far when a skua bird swooped down, knocking Solo to the ground.

She cried and tumbled; then a gust of wind blew her down again, bowling her over and over. The wind blew harder. She rolled and slid along the ice.

The skua bird fought the wind, waiting to dive again.

Solo called for her mother but she was far away, still hurrying to the sea. She struggled to her feet and looked back. The rookery was out of sight.

A bitter wind bowled her over again. And this time she didn't get up. She lay on the ice, weak and shivering.

The skua landed and settled its wings, ready for an easy meal. It reached forward, nipped at Solo's belly and began to tug.

Solo cried out…

… and a passing shape stopped. It hobbled over and lunged at the skua.

Fin was back!

He had finally managed the journey, dragging the fisherman's net the whole way with him.

Weeks later, to Fin and Solo's delight, they heard a familiar sound across the icy wastes – a half-hearted call from Floe.

At once they both replied. And for a wonderful moment they listened to Floe getting closer, calling with joy and disbelief.